■ この絵本の楽しみかた

● 日本文と英文のいずれでも物語を楽しめます。

● 英文は和文に基づいて詩のように書かれています。巻末 Notes を参考にして素晴らしい英詩文を楽しんでください。

● この「日本昔ばなし」の絵はかっての人気絵本「講談社の絵本」全203巻の中から厳選されたものです。

■ About this book

● The story is bilingual, written in both English and Japanese.

● The English is not a direct translation of the Japanese, but rather a retelling of the same story in verse form. Enjoy the English on its own, using the helpful Notes at the back.

● The illustrations are selected from volume 203 of the *Kodansha no ehon* (Kodansha Picture Books) series.

Distributed in the United States by Kodansha America, Inc., 575 Lexington Avenue, New York, N.Y. 10022, and in the United Kingdom and continental Europe by Kodansha Europe Ltd., 95 Aldwych, London WC2B 4JF.
Published by Kodansha International Ltd., 17-14 Otowa 1-chome, Bunkyo-ku, Tokyo 112-8652, and Kodansha America. Inc.

LCC 93-18300
ISBN 4-7700-2099-6

www.thejapanpage.com

和
英
併記

日本昔ばなし

かぐやひめ

THE MOON PRINCESS

え●おだ かんちょう

Illustrations by **Kancho Oda**
Retold by **Ralph F. McCarthy**

KODANSHA INTERNATIONAL
Tokyo · New York · London

むかしむかし，
たけとりのおきなと
よばれる　おじいさんが
いました。

In an ancient
　　bamboo forest
In the mountains
　　of Japan,
Lived an aged
　　bamboo-cutter
And his wife.
　　This kind old man . . .

Once cut down a bamboo glowing
With a light not of this world,
And inside he found a lovely,
Tiny little baby girl.

ある　ひ，　おじいさんが
ふしの　ひかって　いる　たけを　きると，
なかに　かわいい　あかちゃんが　いました。

"Heaven must have sent her to us
So we needn't be alone.
Oh, what joy! To have a little
Fairy princess of our own!
Praise the mystery of life!"
Said the bamboo-cutter's wife.

おじいさんと　おばあさんは
あかちゃんに　かぐやひめと
なまえを　つけました。

Every day from that day on, one
More bamboo he would behold
Shining with a golden light, and
It was always full of gold.

それからは，　おじいさんが
ぴかぴか　ひかる　たけを
きる　たびに，
なかから　おかねが
でて　くるように　なりました。

With the gold they bought their daughter
Silk kimono, smooth and fine.
Like the moon on deep, still water
Did her gentle beauty shine.

In three months she was full grown, with
Eyes like stars that glow at night,
Lighting up the bamboo forest.
And they named her Shining Bright.

かぐやひめは
たいせつに　そだてられて
うつくしい　むすめに
なりました。

Hearing of her dazzling beauty,
People came by day and night
Just to catch a fleeting glimpse of
Lovely Princess Shining Bright.
All the young men smiled and sighed:
"Ah, to make that girl my bride!"

みやこの　わかものたちが
あつまって　きては
「うつくしい　ひめを
　わたしの　つまに
　できるものなら…。」
と，ためいきを　つきました。

15

From the Palace came five suitors,
Princes all, to win her hand,
But she had no wish to marry,
So she told the kind old man:

しかし，かぐやひめは およめに
いく きが ありません。
それでも 5にんの
わかものたちは あきらめないで
けっこんを もうしこみました。
しかたなく かぐやひめは
5にんに ちゅうもんを だして，
のぞみを かなえた ひとの
およめさんに なると いいました。

"Ask Prince Kuramochi to bring me
Jeweled branches from the tree
Growing on a sacred mountain
Far beyond the misty sea.

"There's a ball of many colors
Treasured by the Dragon King:
Tell Prince Otomo that this is
All I ask of him to bring.

くらもちのみこには うみの そこに ある ほうせきを
ちりばめた こえだを, おおとものみゆきには りゅうの
くびに ついた ごしきの たまを, いそのかみまろには
つばめの こやすがいを, と いうように, だれも
みた ことの ない ものばかりを ちゅうもんしました。

"In the belly of the swallow
Is a perfect cowry shell:
Prince Isó shall bring it to me,
With the unharmed bird, as well . . ."

And so on . . . The bamboo-cutter
Gave the five men different tasks.
"Shining Bright," he said, "will marry
He who brings her what she asks."

Prince Kuramochi made a show of
Sailing off across the sea,
But he secretly returned and
Hired some craftsmen for a fee.

"Make a jeweled branch," he told them
With a crafty wink and leer.
"Make it absolutely perfect."
So they did—it took all year!

くらもちのみこは　しょくにんに
にせの　こえだを　つくらせました。

21

Princess Shining Bright believed he'd
Brought the sacred branch, until
All the craftsmen came and shouted:
"Prince Kuramochi owes us still
For the jeweled branch we made!
We won't leave until we're paid!"

かぐやひめは　ほうせきの　こえだを　みて，
びっくりしました。　そこに
しょくにんたちが　きて，いいました。
「てまちんを　まだ　もらって　いません。」
にせもので　ある　ことが
わかって　しまいました。

Prince Otomo set out with his
Bow to find the Dragon King,
Boasting: "Who's afraid of dragons?
They shall feel my arrow's sting!"

おおとものみゆきは
「わたしが　この　やで　りゅうを
　いとめて　みせる。」
と，ゆみやを　もって
ふねに　のりこみました。

Out at sea he met a storm that
Tossed his ship upon the foam.
"Please!" he cried. "Don't let me die! I'll
Hunt no more! I'm going home!"

ところが、　りゅうの　たたりとも　おもえる
あらしに　おそわれました。
「うわー、
　いのちだけは　たすけて　ください。」
おおとものみゆきは
なきだして　しまいました。

27

Prince Isó went to a wise man,
Who said: "Listen to me well:
When the swallow lays her eggs—that's
When you'll find the cowry shell."

So his men rigged up a crane, with
Which they raised the love-obsessed
Prince Isó up to the palace
Roof, where swallows made their nest.

いそのかみまろは, ある おじいさんの
ことばを しんじました。
「こやすがいは,
　つばめが たまごを うむ ときに
　いっしょに うむ ものだ。」
そこで つばめの すの ところに
かごを つるしました。

When he reached inside the nest, his
Hand touched something hard and round.
"That's it, men!" he cried. "I've got it!
Quickly, get me to the ground!"

あるひ，すのなかに
てをつっこむと，
なにかさわりました。
「こやすがいがあったぞー。」

あまりにも　いそいで　おりた
いそのかみまろは，　からだを
いためつけて　しまいました。
5にんの　わかものは
だれひとりとして
のぞみを　かなえる　ことが
できませんでした。

He came down *too* quickly, and he
Sprained his back and hurt his leg.
"Well," he moaned, "at least I've got it!
Look! I've got . . . a *swallow's egg*?

So it went.
    The princess never
Wed, but spent
    four happy years
With the kind old
    couple, till one
Night they found her
    shedding tears,
Gazing at
    the misty moon,
Whispering:
    "Too soon! Too soon!"

やがて，　かぐやひめは
つきを　みる　たびに
かなしい　かおを
するように　なりました。
そして　8がつの
じゅうごやが　ちかづくと,
つきを　みては　なみだを
ながすように　なりました。

"What is it, our darling daughter?
What is it that makes you weep?"

"Mother, Father, there's a secret
That I can no longer keep.
I'm a princess of the City
On the Moon. There was a war.
I was sent here to escape a
Danger that exists no more.

おじいさんと　おばあさんは，
なみだの　わけを　ききました。
「わたくしは　つきから　きた
てんにょなのです。
こんどの　8がつの
じゅうごやには
かえらなければ　なりません。」

おどろいた　おじいさんは
いいました。
「へいたいたちに
　まもらせよう。」

"On the fifteenth night of August,
When the moon is full and bright,
People of the Moon are coming.
I must leave you on that night!"

"No! I simply won't allow it!"
Cried the bamboo-cutter. "Why
Should I let them take you? I shall
Hire a thousand samurai!"

On the fifteenth night of August,
Samurai stood with their bows
On the roof and in the garden
As the full moon slowly rose.

いよいよ　じゅうごやの
ばんに　なりました。
へいたいたちは　つきが　のぼると，
ゆみに　やを　つがえて
まちかまえました。

Shining Bright was in her chamber,
Doors and windows bolted tight,
When, at midnight, in the moonbeams
There appeared a cloud of light.
Soon the sky was bright as noon,
Lit by People of the Moon.

やがて あたりが あかるく なり,
そらから くもに のった
てんにょたちが おりて きました。

41

Bathed in that unearthly light, the
Samurai were paralyzed.
They could neither shoot nor speak, and
One by one they closed their eyes.

「それっ，　きたぞー。」
へいたいたちは　いさみたちましたが，
どう　した　ことか，　だれもが　みうごきが
できなく　なって　しまいました。
そして　ひめを　かくして　いた
へやの　かぎが　しぜんに　はずれ，
とが　あいて　しまいました。

By itself, the door slid open.
Out stepped Princess Shining Bright.
"Dear old parents, we may never
Meet again. Tonight's the night."

"Darling daughter, please don't leave us!"
Cried the bamboo-cutter's wife.

"Stay!" the bamboo-cutter pleaded.
"You mean more to us than life!"

"I will not forget your love,"
Said the princess from above.

「おわかれする　ときが　まいりました。
　この　きものを　どうぞ
　わたくしだと　おもって　ください。」
かぐやひめは　なみだを
ながして　いいました。

45

With one last farewell she turned and
Stepped on to the cloud of light.
Then it rose up to the heavens
Till it vanished in the night.

さいごの　わかれを　つげると，
かぐやひめは　ばしゃに　のり，
よぞらの　なかに　きえて　いきました。

47

Notes   かぐやひめ♦The Moon Princess♦

p.5	an ancient bamboo forest 古い竹林　aged 年とった　bamboo-cutter 竹とり
p.6	glowing 光かがやく　with a light not of this world この世のものでない光で
p.9	Heaven 天　To have 〜 〜をもらうとは　Praise ほめたたえよ
p.10	one more bamboo またひとつの竹を　full of gold 黄金でいっぱいの
p.12	smooth and fine なめらかですばらしい　Like the moon on deep, still water 深い、静かな水面にうつった月のように　did her gentle beauty shine 姫のおだやかな美しさは照り輝いた　full grown 大人になった　with eyes like stars 星のような目の　glow at night 夜に輝く　Shining Bright かぐや姫
p.14	Hearing of her dazzling beauty まばゆい美しさをききつけて　just to catch a fleeting glimpse of〜 〜を一目見ようと　sighed ため息をついた　bride 花嫁
p.17	suitors 求婚者　to win her hand 彼女と結婚しようとして
p.18	jeweled branches 宝石のついた枝　sacred 神聖な　far beyond the misty sea 霧のはるか彼方の　treasured by 〜 〜の大切にしている　this is all I ask of him to 〜 〜することしか彼には求めません
p.19	In the belly of the swallow ツバメのおなかに　cowry shell 子安貝の貝から
p.20	made a show of sailing off 航海に出たふりをした　craftsmen 職人　for a fee 金を払って　with a crafty wink and leer ずるそうにウインクして目をそばめて　absolutely perfect 完全完ぺきに　So they did 職人はそのとおりにした
p.22	until ところが最後に　owes us still for 〜 私たちにまだ〜の借りがある
p.24	set out でかけた　bow 決意　boasting 誇りながら　Who's afraid of dragons? 竜がこわいものか　They shall feel my arrow's sting わしの矢の味わわせてやる
p.27	tossed his ship upon the foam 彼の船を波間にほんろうした
p.29	lays her eggs 卵を産む　that's when そのときこそ　rigged up a crane 彼を持ち上げるものを急いでつくった　with which それで　love-obsessed 恋わずらいの
p.30	hard and round 堅くまるい　That's it これだ　get me to the ground 下に降ろせ
p.33	came down too quickly 降りるのが速すぎた　sprained 痛めた　moaned うめいた
p.34	So it went. このような結果になった　shedding tears 涙を流して　Gazing at 〜 〜をながめて　whispering ささやきながら　Too soon! 早すぎます
p.36	What is it that makes you weep? いったいなぜおまえは泣くのか　a secret that I can no longer keep もう隠せない秘密　war 戦争　to escape a danger that exists no more 危険をのがれるためでしたが、その危険はもうありません
p.37	I simply won't allow it わしは許さぬ　Why should I let them take you? おまえを連れていかせる理由はない
p.40	in her chamber 自分の部屋に　bolted tight 厳重にかんぬきがかけられた　in the moonbeams 月の光線の中に　as noon 昼のように　lit by 〜 〜によって照らされて
p.42	Bathed in that unearthly light そのこの世ならぬ光を浴びて　were paralyzed マヒした　one by one 一人また一人と
p.44	By itself ひとりでに　out stepped 歩みでた　pleaded 懇願した　You mean more to us than life! お前は私たちには命より大切なのだ　from above 上の方から
p.47	With one last farewell 最後に別れを告げると

（佐藤公俊）

●和英併記●日本昔ばなし　かぐやひめ

おだ　かんちょう／ラルフ F. マッカーシー

発行日　1996年 9月27日　第 1 刷発行
　　　　2001年11月26日　第 7 刷発行

発行者　野間佐和子

発行所　講談社インターナショナル株式会社
　　　　〒112-8652 東京都文京区音羽1-17-14
　　　　〔電話〕03(3944)6493
　　　　ホームページ http://www.kodansha-intl.co.jp

協　力　講談社児童局
印　刷　大日本印刷株式会社
製　本　黒柳製本株式会社

© Kodansha International 1993 Printed in Japan
ISBN 4-7700-2099-6